DOCTOR QUACK

Geraldine McCaughrean

illustrated by Ross Collins

Hodder Children's Books

a division of Hodder Headline Limited

Text copyright © 2003 Geraldine McCaughrean
Illustrations copyright © 2003 Ross Collins

First published in Great Britain in 2003 by Hodder Children's Books

This paperback edition published by Hodder Children's Books in 2003

A Catalogue record for this book is available from the British Library

ISBN 0 340 86606 3

Printed and bound in Great Britain by Clays Ltd, St Ives plc

The paper and board used in this paperback by Hodder Children's Books are
natural recyclable products made from wood grown in sustainable forests.
The manufacturing processes conform to the environmental regulations
of the country of origin.

Hodder Children's Books
A division of Hodder Headline Limited
338 Euston Road, London, NW1 3BH

For Miranda

Contents

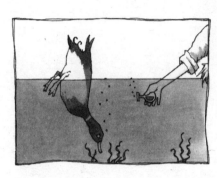

Chapter One
Ill Will

"Listen! Gather round! This is your lucky day!"

Benedick set down his pack at the top of the town hall steps. In his harlequin suit he was as bright and sharp as a handful of diamonds, but close-to you might have seen that his cuffs were ragged and his buttons were loose. For a doctor, Benedick was very young and rather down-at-heel, but his voice was very loud: "Today only and never again, the great Doctor Benedick has come to town!"

It was market day – early morning – and people were arriving in the square with donkeys and dogs, baskets of duck eggs and chickens head-down. No one else had begun yet to cry their wares, so they looked up at the boy on the town hall steps.

"A Doctor? Where? Where?" they asked.

"Here! Here!" said Benedick. "*I* am Doctor Benedick, healer to princes and princesses, lords and ladies, earls and ear-lobes! Roll up! Roll up and buy a medicine for every illness!"

People drifted over towards him – a woman with a goat, a boy with a goose. Everyone who has ever been ill knows what a cure is worth.

Out from the pack came a greenish bottle full of greenish liquid. Benedick held it like a green duck egg, like a handful of precious emeralds. "This medicine," he said, "will cure coughs and colds and collywobbles. This medicine will heal hives, hiccups and whooping cough!"

But the woman with the goat wrinkled up her nose in a very goat-like expression: "We've seen your kind before," she seemed to say.

Quack doctors had come to town many times in the past and sold them oil of figs in green bottles, calling it a cure-all. It wasn't. So nobody bought Benedick's bottle of marvellous medicine. They did not trust him.

"Why, only last week one of your sort came here and took our hard-earned money. Quack! Quack! You are nothing but a quack doctor," and they showered him with green sprouts.

Benedick knew what they meant. Back in his own home town, across the mountains, a man had come selling medicine in much the same way.

Benedick's father was very, very ill with the purple plague. "Past hope," said the priest. "Past recovery," said the neighbours. "No one recovers from the purple plague."

But this man – Doctor Do-Wonders he called himself – swaggered into the house, raising his stove-pipe hat, tapping his nose. He closed his one blue eye and, from the doorway of the bedroom, examined Benedick's father with the black one. "Aha, I see!" he said. "Yes, yes. For a hundred fleurons I have just the medicine for this ailment. Sadly I have to leave town tonight, but bring me one hundred gold fleurons by sundown, and the cure is yours. How lucky that I came along when I did!"

One hundred fleurons? He might as well have asked for the moon to dip in his tea. There were not seven fleurons in the whole house.

"Sell the cow, Benedick!" his mother said. "Sell the forks and spoons! Sell grandpa's

spurs – the ones he left us. Sell
my thick woollen coat!"

So Benedick opened the
house window facing on to the
street and, all day long, he sold
the family goods: knick-knacks
and furniture, clothes and the
clock. By the end of the day he
had become rather good at selling
things.

"What an excellent little tradesman you are, Benedick!" said all the neighbours. "Just like a pedlar!" said his brothers and sisters. "Almost convincing," said the priest.

Even so, he had raised only sixty-one fleurons.

"Quick, Benedick! Sell the house!" said his mother.

"But Mama! Where will we live if we sell the house?"

"What does it matter?" she cried in return. "So long as your father gets well!"

Benedick crossed the market square, remembering. As he did so, he took off his green hat and put on a yellow one. Over his harlequin suit, he swung a yellow cloak (though close-to you might have seen that it was really last week's newspaper). Then he jumped up on to a big barrel of beer and loudly said, "Today only and never again! The brilliant and famous Wizard Benedick has come to town!"

Chapter Two
Trouble

The people passing through the town gate were intrigued. "Who? Where?" they asked.

The market place was busier now. Hammers banged as the tradesmen set up their stalls. The guards in front of the palace doors said, "Make less noise! The King is sleeping!" but no one took any notice. Every market day the guards said the same thing.

"Me! Here!" said Benedick. "I am the Wizard Benedick, magic-maker to mayors and marquises, dukes and duchesses, counts and counties! Roll up! Roll up and see the potion of all potions, the lotion of all lotions!"

Out from the pack came a

yellowish bottle full of a greenish liquid. He held it like a hen's egg, like a handful of precious topaz. Then he shouted: "This potion will protect you from demons, scare off ghosts and banish nightmares!"

Now, anyone who has ever hurried past a churchyard or heard bumps in the night, or woken up screaming at midnight, knows how fearful demons and ghosts and nightmares can be. But still nobody bought his magic potion. They had seen quack magicians before, and they did not believe in mumbo-jumbo magic.

"Quack! Quack!" they all called. "You are nothing but a quack wizard," and they pelted him with yellow lentils. "Why, only last year one of your kind came here and took our hard-earned money."

Poor Benedick. But he could understand how they felt.

Back in his own home town, across the mountains, he had worked without rest or sleep to save his father's life; to raise the money for Doctor Do-Wonders' marvellous medicine.

"You were lucky to catch me," Doctor Do-Wonders said, polishing his tall stove-pipe hat with the cuff of his jacket as he prepared to leave town. "Do you have the money?"

"We sold the forks and we sold the carpet!" sobbed Benedick. "We sold the pictures and we sold the cat! We sold the beds and then, when that wasn't enough, we sold the house . . . but this is all we could raise!" and he held out ninety-six jingling, golden fleurons.

Doctor Do-Wonders scowled
and rubbed his stubbly chin.
"Some people might try to take
advantage of my generous and
trusting nature." Suddenly his
face brightened. "But I can see
you are telling me the truth.
You have an honest face, boy.
I'm a fool to myself, but do you
know what I am going to do?
I am going to do you a kindness.
You can owe me the other four
fleurons, and pay me back the
next time I am in town. I trust
you." And he held out a phial
of brightly-coloured liquid.

Benedick took hold of
it between shaking hands.
"Thank you, sir! Oh, thank you!

Thank you! Thank you!"

Benedick crossed the market
square. He took off his yellow
hat and put on a blue one. He
screwed up his yellow newspaper
(although first he tore out a
picture from the front page and
pushed it tenderly inside his
shirt). Then he turned the jacket
of his harlequin suit inside out so
that only the blue lining showed.

Out of the pack came a blue
bottle filled with greenish liquid.
He held it like a blue lark's egg,
like a handful of precious sapphires.

Balancing on a pile of corn
sacks, he bellowed: "Today only
and never again! The amazing,
the astonishing Alchemist

Benedick, wonder-worker to czars and czarinas, to wazirs a wasn'ts! Here is something to change your life. Here is something to change *anything*. I hold in my hand the Essence of Change. It can change grass into brass, mould into gold, dice into mice, sheep into ships!"

Now, anyone who has ever put their hand into a pocket and pulled out a penny, hoping it would be a shilling, wishes for a change in their life. Anyone who has ever looked in the mirror one morning and seen a face like a sheep, with bat-ears and crows-feet, bug-eyes and owl-jowls, knows what *they* would give for a change.

But nobody bought Benedick's blue essence. They had seen quack alchemists before, and they knew that change does not come easily. They did not believe in silly pseudo-sciences. "Quack! Quack!" they all called. "You are nothing but a quack alchemist! Just last month one of your kind came here and cheated us," and they bombarded him with blue grapes.

Poor Benedick. But he could understand how they felt.

It took Benedick two days to catch up with Doctor Do-Wonders. "You lied," he said. "Your medicine was nothing but lemon juice. My father is dead. We have nothing left. Everything is sold. The cat tried to come home but there was no home for her to come to. You have ruined us."

Doctor Do-Wonders shrugged and turned away. "It serves you right for being so trusting. A man must make a living . . . But then I suppose you will find that out, now your father is dead." And, as the quack doctor slung his pack over his shoulder and walked on, whistling, Benedick could hear all those gold fleurons clashing and jangling.

Benedick crossed the market square towards a statue of the King. He took off his yellow hat and put on a red one. He

turned his harlequin trousers
inside out so that their red
lining showed. Out of the pack
came a red bottle filled with
greenish liquid. He held it like
a palmful of wine, or blood, or
precious rubies.

He climbed astride the
statue and whispered very softly,
"Here today and gone tomorrow!
I hold in my hand something
to heal your heart and grant
your wishes! I, Don Benedick,
have brought you the . . . Elixir
of Love.

"One sip and you will be
adored. Girls? The boys will faint
at your feet. Boys? The girls will
swoon at the sight of you. Even
dogs will come when you whistle.

Even the most . . ."

"Get down from the King's statue this instant!"

It was the Royal Guard, with drawn swords and angry faces.

"Get down! You are under arrest!"

Chapter Three
The King's Judgement

The guards grabbed Benedick and carried him into the royal castle, into the presence of the King and Queen and the Princess, who were eating their royal breakfast.

"Who do we have here?" asked the King.

"Another quack, your Majesty," said the Captain of the Guard, "just like the last one. He tried to sell a marvellous medicine, a magic potion to scare off ghosts, an essence for transforming things, and an elixir of love."

Benedick's pack was emptied on to the floor. Out fell the four bottles: green and yellow and blue and red.

"What's this? What's this? What's this?" asked the King,

sniffing them each in turn.
"Phew! They smell like pond
water!"

"It was not the smell I was
selling," said Benedick. "I was
selling the magic. The smell
comes free."

The Princess hid a smile
behind her napkin. The Queen
jabbed a spoon into the jam.

The King sliced the top off his boiled egg with a sharp silver knife. "We have met your kind before, oh yes! Every market day quacks come to town, and every market day I throw them into my dungeon. Take him away!"

"Quite right," groaned Benedick sinking into a chair and wiping his forehead. "You are quite right to try and protect your people. I admire and respect you for it. I know it is useless to protest."

The Princess frowned and put down her toast.

Benedick gave a few short, hacking coughs. "But please – just before you lock me up – let me take one sip from the green bottle! I feel very ill."

Then he fell to the floor, gurgling.

"What's the matter with him?" squeaked the Queen.

"The Plague. It's the Purple Plague," gasped Benedick. "But give me the GREEN bottle and in a day or two, I shall be . . . *urghk*."

There was uproar. The Queen clutched the Princess Clematis; the King stood on his throne. The Captain of the Guard threw open all the windows in the room. Then he kicked the green bottle across the floor, and Benedick scooped it up with trembling fingers. He drank a sip of the medicine and pulled a face.

"I'm sorry," he whispered,

bowing his head to the Princess. "Magic is always a little hard to swallow."

Then the Royal Guard threw him into the deepest dungeon and left him there to die.

Everyone dies of the Purple Plague.

Chapter Four
The Medicine

Down deep among the foundations of the palace, Benedick sprawled among the dirty straw of the King's dungeons. The guards clanged shut the door. A thousand cockroaches shivered with delight at the sight of him.

Waiting until the sound of the guard's footsteps had faded to a silence, Benedick sat up, laughing. It was not the worst thing that could happen to a boy. The worst thing had happened long before.

He began to peer about the cell. There was no light, but for a trickle coming through the keyhole as from a tap left dripping. That was a shame. Now he would not be able to console himself by looking at his newspaper picture of Princess Clematis. It was usually the last thing he did each night before going to sleep.

Now, of course, he had seen the real thing: the Princess in person, her teaspoon poised over the golden heart of a boiled egg. What he would have given to be that egg! There again, the real Princess had been frowning at him, whereas the Princess in the newspaper picture was always smiling her brightest smile. Sometimes photographs are better than the real thing.

Something in the cell moved and it was larger than a cockroach. *Rats!* thought

Benedick and shuddered. The noise came again. A voice enquired, "What did you do, then, to be joining me for breakfast among the spiders?"

"Who's there?"

"Judge Fair-Do's the name," said the voice. "Imprisoned here by a terrible miscarriage of justice. I should never have expected any better of them. There is no justice to be had in this sort of two-donkey, one-drain, no-hope town full of paltry poultry farmers! Do you know, they locked me up because of *the colour of my eyes*?"

"That's an outrage and I'm very sorry to hear it," said Benedick. "Perhaps I can help."

Out of the darkness there came a snort of disdain. "I hardly think so, young man. More probably, *I* can help *you* – with my knowledge of the law. Do you have any money to pay for my services?"

Benedick thought for a moment. "I'm afraid I have no small change on me . . ."

"Huh! Just another ragamuffin beggar."

". . . only a banknote for one thousand fleurons."

"My fee exactly!" said Judge Fair-Do. "Hand it over, and I shall represent you at your trial. You certainly need the benefit of my great legal mind. I shall blind the court with my genius!

I shall bamboozle it with my scholarship! I shall banjax it with my eloquence! In short, I shall have you and me out of here in a twinkling."

Benedick reached into his tunic and brought out the newspaper cutting of Princess Clematis. He hated to part with it, but freedom is freedom. In the dark, their hands clashed. The square of paper crinkled like a banknote. Then it was gone – into the darker darkness of Judge Fair-Do's pocket.

"I hardly like to mention it, sir," said Benedick, "but you may need a friend at your own trial. Now, for just one hundred fleurons, I would witness to your good character, your honesty, your fair-mindedness. There is no light in here, or you could see what an honest face I have. People only have to look at me to believe what I say."

The Judge hesitated. "Hmmm."

"Want to hear a sample?" said Benedick. *"Ever since I was a child I have known this good man – this excellent, this generous Judge Fair-Do! Why, when my family was in desperate trouble, who came to our aid? Judge Fair-Do! I don't know what would have become of us but for good old Judge Fair-Do! I mean to say . . ."*

"All right, all right. Enough!" There was a scraping sound of a pack being dragged across the cell floor, the jingle of buckles being undone. "Here are one hundred fleurons. I shall be your lawyer and you shall be my character witness . . . Do you have anything on you to drink?"

"I did have, sir, but I'm afraid the King confiscated all my bottles," said Benedick.

Somewhere the drip of water made a hollow, echoing noise. Somewhere a nest of mice clambered over one another in their sleep. Somewhere, in the palace overhead, the King was singing in his bath. The sound of singing was remarkably loud in the deep, dark dungeon.

"Is there a fireplace in here?" Benedick asked the Judge.

"Pah! How should I know! A High Court Judge does not concern himself with *fireplaces.* There's no fire, I know that. Brrrr. I'm frozen!"

Benedick got up and felt his way around the walls of the cell until he found (as he had expected) a fireplace. There was no fire lit in it, of course, but it was wide and deep. Benedick ducked under the mantlepiece, stuck his head up the chimney and began to shout:

> *"Ghouls and ghosts awake, arise,*
> *Take this castle by surprise.*
> *Let us horrid, hooting things*
> *Show them what we think of kings!"*

"What *are* you doing?" demanded Judge Fair-Do. "Are you mad? Am I locked up in here with a madman?"

Benedick said nothing, but an hour later he stuck his head up the chimney and shouted the selfsame words:

"Ghouls and ghosts awake, arise,
Take this castle by surprise.
Let us horrid, hooting things
Show them what we think of kings!"

Feeling his way around the cell floor, he found a length of chain and clanked it. He found a bucket of something evil-smelling, and banged on it with a shoe. He found the Judge's tin plate and spoon and banged them together, too. He pulled up a floor tile and smashed it against the wall. He found the palace water pipes and scraped them with a piece of broken tile.

"Stop that! *Stop that!* Are you completely mad?" demanded the Judge, but Benedick only stuck his head up the chimney and sang:

> *"Ghouls and ghosts awake, arise,*
> *Take this castle by surprise.*
> *Let us horrid, hooting things*
> *Show them what we think of kings!"*

After two whole days, the jailer came back, with the town undertaker and a cardboard coffin. As he opened the door, the

light of his torch was blindingly
bright. He shone it directly into
Benedick's face. Then he dropped
the torch on the floor.

"Mercy me! You got better!
We came here to get the body for
burying, and here you are alive
and blinking! How is that? No one

ever gets better from the Purple Plague!"

"*Purple Plague?*" shrieked Judge Fair-Do and crawled away to the far end of the cell.

"It was just lucky that I had my medicine on me," said Benedick humbly.

"That must be truly wonderful medicine!" gasped the jailer.

"Wonderful, yes," agreed Benedick. "Please tell the King. When he knows that my medicine was genuine, he is sure to let me go."

Chapter Five
The Nightmare Solution

"Oh, but the King has shut himself up in his bedroom," said the jailer. "He is too afraid to come out, because of the ghosts."

"*Ghosts?*" echoed Judge Fair-Do from the far end of the cell.

"Yeah. Day and night he hears them howling round about the palace. I've heard them too!"

"Ah yes. I thought so," said Benedick gravely. "I thought I felt an evil presence as soon as I set foot in this palace. You must tell the King: go to my pack and take out the YELLOW bottle! Yellow, do you hear? Tell him to drink what's in it. It will protect him from ghosts and ghouls. Didn't I say so when I first came to town?"

"Hmmm," said the jailer, and clanged shut the door.

But he *did* tell the King.

"The prisoner arrested on market day says you should drink from the YELLOW bottle, Your Majesty. Says it will protect you from ghosts and ghouls and all manner of nightmares."

"The prisoner in the harlequin suit?" said Princess Clematis, who was cutting up the King's lunch for him into bite-sized pieces. "But I thought . . . Is he still alive, then?"

"Oo yeah, milady," said the jailer. "He's as fit as a ferret, on account of that green medicine he drank."

The King stopped blowing bubbles in his malted milk and

hiccuped. "A cure for the Purple Plague, eh? . . . Still, we only have his word for that."

Twenty times the King chewed on each bite-sized piece of his dinner and, while he chewed, he thought. At the end of the meal, he sent for Benedick's pack and searched it for the yellow bottle. Holding his nose, he swallowed down the potion inside (even though it did taste like pond water).

Three days later, Benedick was still sitting in his prison cell. He thought it was time to ask Judge Fair-Do when he might hope for his release.

"I am still preparing the

legal paperwork. People never realize how much paperwork there is in the legal profession. Just as soon as it is ready, I shall have you out of here."

"I'm surprised you can see to work without one glint of light," said Benedick.

"Oh, I can read by touch," said the Judge. "I learned the art at Scanderdifitus University when I was studying for my thirteenth degree . . . I have to say, boy, I am extremely relieved that you have stopped all that shouting and singing and clanking and banging. It was starting to fray my nerves."

"My throat got sore," said Benedick.

Just then, the prison door opened and the jailer shone his torch in Benedick's face. "The King wants to see you," he said.

"Not ME?" demanded Judge Fair-Do.

"Not you," said the jailer.

"I see you recovered from the Purple Plague," said the King, talking down his nose.

"I did, I did," said Benedick. "What a lucky boy I am! I can hardly believe that Your Majesty thought to ask after a young nobody like me. In my experience, princes and princesses, lords and ladies, earls and ear-lobes do not take much interest in mere travelling doctors, especially when they are young. Might I ask – did you sleep well, Your Majesty?"

"I did," said the King suspiciously. "I have not heard a single ghost since I drank from the yellow bottle."

"You see? Didn't I say as

much when I first came to town?
I said that potion of mine could
banish demons, ghosts and
nightmares! I, Wizard Benedick,
magic-maker to mayors and
marquises, dukes and duchesses,
counts and counties, sell only the
finest potions! . . . So, can I go

now?" asked Benedick.

He picked up his pack and headed hopefully for the door. He could not help noticing that someone was eating toast behind the tapestry wall-hanging; crumbs were dropping down on to the tips of a pair of satin shoes. (The shoes were all that showed, sticking out from below the tapestry.)

"Not so fast!" said the King. "What about this BLUE bottle? Your so-called Essence of Change. Before you go, won't you show me *that* one at work?"

Benedick stopped, with his hand on the doorknob.

The King grinned grimly, thinking, "Aha! Now I have

caught him out, the young villain!"

The person behind the tapestry thought so too.

Perhaps they were both right.

Chapter Six
A Bit of a Change

Benedick thought for a moment. "Show you my Essence of Change? Certainly, Your Majesty," he said.

He took the blue bottle of greenish liquid and went to the window.

"I, Alchemist Benedick, wonder-worker to czars and czarinas, to wazirs and wasn'ts, will now transform a few of Your Majesty's loyal subjects . . . if you don't have any objection, I mean."

"Transform them?" said the King. "How d'you mean, 'transform' them?"

The Queen suddenly emerged from an ottoman treasure chest behind the throne.

Her hair was woolly with blanket fluff. "Yes! What does he mean, 'transform' our subjects?"

The Princess, too intrigued to be hidden, stepped out from behind the tapestry.

"Really, Clematis!" said the Queen. "How often do I have to tell you not to go eavesdropping on things that don't concern you!"

"Even so, Alchemist Benedick," said Princess Clematis in her low, husky voice. "What exactly will you transform them into?"

Benedick bowed low to the Princess then, opening the French windows, stepped out on to the balcony. The market square below was thronged with people. The

market was at its busiest.
Housewives and horse-dealers
jostled with beggars and buskers.
Striped stalls stood in serried
rows selling cheeses and ferrets
and herbs and buckets and
marmalades.

Out of his pack he drew the
blue bottle full of greenish liquid.
"I think I shall change them
into . . . now, let me see . . ."
Benedick drew out the cork with
a flourish and looked about him,
as if for possibilities. A skein of
geese flew, in arrow formation,
across the sunny sky. ". . . into
DUCKS, my lady. Into ducks!"

So saying, he sprinkled some
of the essence over the people
below.

Feeling wet drops falling on their heads, the people in the market square said, "*Urgh*," and wiped their faces. They looked up and saw Benedick waving to them from the balcony of the King's palace.

"*Quack!*" they shouted, angrily. "*Quack! Quack!*"

Benedick stepped back inside, before they began throwing things.

"Amazing!" said the Queen.

Benedick crossed to another window and stepped out on to a second balcony. Once again he sprinkled the blue-green liquor over the crowds below. Once again the people looked up and shook their fists.

"Quack!" they roared furiously. "*Quack!* QUACK! QUACK!"

Chapter Seven
The Elixir
of Love

"Unbelievable!" said the Princess
Clematis, hiding her face with
both hands.

"Hmph," said the King
dubiously. "There is still the
matter of the RED bottle." He
smiled a nasty smile. "Your so-
called 'Elixir of Love'."

"Keep it, do!" said Benedick,
struggling with the door-handle.
"Call it a free sample."

"Not so fast," said the King,
holding up the red bottle of
greenish liquid. "How am I to
know if this is genuine elixir or
half a cup of pondwater?"

Benedick's eyes grew
very large and round. "Your
Majesty! Was I not cured of
the Purple Plague by drinking

from the green bottle?"

"Hmmm," said the King.

"And didn't you drink the potion in the *yellow* bottle, and didn't it drive away all those noisy, hooting ghosts and demons and nightmares?"

"Uh-huh," said the King, drumming his fingers.

"And you *heard* him turn our subjects into ducks!" cried the Queen, ". . . though I'm a little worried about them. Can they be changed back, please, Alchemist?"

"Oh, it wears off," Benedick assured her. "Pretty soon they will be quite their old selves."

Clearly the King still had his doubts, for he suddenly wrenched out the cork and drank from the small red bottle. A terrible silence fell over the royal court, as well as a slight smell of pondwater.

"Aha!" said the King after some time, and then again, "Aha! I knew it!"

Benedick did not wait to find out what the King knew. He dropped his pack and ran.

What? Do you think he ran away – out of the doors and down all those stairs, fighting his way past the Royal Guard and sixteen kinds of guard dog? He would have been mad even to try it.

No, Benedick ran the *other* way. He ran the whole length of the royal court, his eyes bulging, his hands clasped over his heart. *"Oh Your Majesty! Your dear, handsome, adorable, wonderful Majesty!"* And he flung his arms around the royal shoulders and planted a kiss squarely on the royal mouth.

"*Pblshlagh!*" said the King. "Guards! Guards! Get him off me!"

The Queen forgot to scream.

80

Princess Clematis remembered only just in time not to laugh. The guards (when they got over their surprise) grabbed Benedick by his ragged jacket, wrestled him to the ground and sat on him. For as long as he was able, he went on kissing the King's stockings, robe and boots.

"I'm sorry! I'm sorry!" he wailed. "I don't know what came over me! All of a sudden I couldn't help myself! It's the elixir! I blame the elixir! It's just too powerful!" He beamed and beamed with every crease of his face and every twinkle in his blue eyes.

But the King only spluttered with rage. "Now I KNOW you are

a quack and a trickster! Do you really expect me to believe your flim-flam-doodle? NOBODY falls in love with me! Nobody even *likes* me!"

"Oh, but Godfrith, dear . . ." the Queen protested.

The King was in no mood to listen. "Take him away! Oh, I see through his little trick! To persuade me that the elixir works, he runs and hugs me and swears that he loves me. What kind of fool does he take me for?"

"Er . . ." said Benedick.

"The boy is a rogue and a rascal. That's all there is to it. Take him away and drown him in the moat!" commanded the King.

The guards stood up. Where

they had been sitting, Benedick lay like a squashed marshmallow.

"But what if HE were to drink it?" asked Princess Clematis with a snooty sneer. "You should make him drink his own potion. *That* would prove it once and for all!"

Meanwhile, Benedick lay on the floor and thought of all the people who loved him.

Back in his home town, across the mountains, there was his mother. There were his brothers and sisters. There was Granny Myfanwy. Here, though, there was no one. He was all alone in a town that hated him.

"If your elixir works," said the King, "I will instantly love you. That's correct, isn't it?"

"Er . . ." Benedick gulped.

"If you are lucky, I *might* even love you enough to let you go," sneered the King. "So go ahead. Drink it."

Benedick thought of the liquid in the red bottle. He thought and thought, but no bright idea came to his rescue. So he took the bottle, held his nose, and drank it down.

Chapter Eight
Unfair-Do

It tasted awful. A piece of pondweed stuck in his throat and made him cough. The King drummed his fingers on the arm of his throne.

For a long time, precisely nothing happened.

Then the door swung open and the jailer entered with a nervous bow. "Begging your pardon, Majesty, but the prisoner is asking about his witness."

"What witness?" said the King.

"Which prisoner?" asked the Queen.

The jailer reminded them about Judge Fair-Do, pining away in the darkness of the dungeon. Up until then, they had forgotten all about him.

"Bring him up!" commanded the King. "We can try both of the impostors together!"

When the light of day shone on Judge Fair-Do, it showed a middle-aged man of medium height with mousy hair under his moth-eaten wig. He had one blue eye and one black one. As he glanced around the room his

black eye fell on Benedick and lingered there, uneasily, as if there was something unpleasantly familiar about the boy. Benedick returned the look with a wink and a broad, beaming smile.

So the judge brushed himself clean of cobwebs and pursed his lips up very small. "I have been done a great wrong!" he declared. "It is really quite intolerable that a man of my standing—"

"Read out the charge!" commanded the King.

"This cheat took money from people by pretending he was a High Court Judge, Your Majesty!" said the jailer (who had parted with ten fleurons to Judge Fair-Do and regretted it very much).

Judge Fair-Do laid both hands over his heart and gasped with horror. "How can a man be condemned for being himself! I AM a High Court Judge! That boy knows exactly who I am, as he will tell you!"

All eyes turned on Benedick, who smiled shyly and bowed. "It's true, sire," he said. "I can bear witness to this man's character."

Judge Fair-Do grinned like a well-fed cat and held the lapels of his dusty robe. "Tell them, boy! Tell them!"

Chapter Nine
The Picture of Honesty

"Even in the dark of the Royal dungeon, I recognized that splendid voice of his!" Benedick declared. "This man's name is Doctor Do-Wonders. He came to our village when I was a little boy and my father was sick, and he brought with him this *wonderful* cure! We sold the forks and we sold the carpet. We sold the pictures and we sold the cat. We sold the beds and then, when that wasn't enough, we sold the house to raise the price of that *wonderful* medicine. Of course, it was only lemon juice, and my father still died, but I learned so *much* from this marvellous man!

"In fact I never forgot the

words he spoke to me when we parted: 'It serves you right for being so trusting, boy,' he said. 'A man must make a living.'

"From that day to this, I have tried to follow in his footsteps, always hoping to meet with him again one day and show him how . . . *grateful* I am!"

The room was so silent that the cuckoo in the clock could be heard preening its feathers.

"Lies! All lies!" cried Judge Fair-Do at last. "Will you take the word of this . . . this . . . little *quack* . . . against the solemn oath of a High Court Judge?!"

The King drummed his fingers on the arm of his chair. The Queen dabbed at her eyes with a handkerchief. Princess Clematis turned her face away.

"He is right," said the King sadly. "It is his word against yours, your word against his."

"Oh, please!" said Benedick, spreading his palms and smiling brightly. "Please don't think I hold a grudge! How can I blame the good Doctor for something that happened such a long time ago? No, no!"

"No, no?" said the King.

"No, no?" said Judge Fair-Do.

"No, no?" said the Queen.

"No, no?" said Princess Clematis.

"No, no!" said Benedick cheerfully. "I am only angry that, while we shared a dungeon deep down below here, he filched my dearest possession."

"He did?" said the Queen.

"He did?" said the King.

"I never!" protested Judge Fair-Do. His hands flew guiltily to his pack. Then he smiled a smirking smile. "And what exactly was that?" he sneered.

"Yes, what was it?" asked Princess Clematis in a whisper.

Benedick blushed and hung his head and dug the toe of one boot into the King's carpet. "My photograph of the Princess Clematis."

The King gaped. The Queen gasped. The Princess stared at Benedick with round green eyes.

"Not a real photograph, I

don't mean," said Benedick
hastily. "A newspaper cutting.
Every night before sleeping, I
used to take it out and look at it –
that smile, those eyes, those two
locks of hair curling down in front
of her ears . . ."

Benedick broke off and there
was such a silence in the big room
that the mice could be heard
sharpening their whiskers.

"Is this true?" asked the
King, turning to Judge Fair-Do.

"Not a word of it! Search
me! You will find nothing
in my pockets but the fees I
have earned in the course of
my law work!" His face was
smug with certainty. For once
in his life, Doctor Do-Nothing

was being accused of something he really had not done.

"Why should he want to steal a picture of me?" asked the Princess, with understandable curiosity.

Benedick shrugged. "Perhaps he admires you as much as I do."

"Rubbish! Nonsense! Balderdash!" exclaimed the other prisoner, chortling at the absurdity of the idea.

The Queen bridled. The King bristled. Even the Princess (who was not a vain girl) looked as if someone had trodden on her smile.

"If it wasn't love, then," suggested Benedick, "perhaps he came here to kidnap her."

At the mere thought of such a terrible crime, the Royal Guard pounced on Judge Fair-Do and turned out his pockets and there among the trouser fluff, they found the scrap of yellowing newspaper.

"B-b-b-but I thought it

was a thousand-fleuron note!"
The Judge's voice echoed back
along the corridor as the guards
dragged him away to the
dungeons.

Chapter Ten
The Secret Ingredient

When the guards came back, the King pointed at Benedick and said, "Take *him* away, too. I'm sorry, lad, but I will not have quacks in my city, and that's that!"

Benedick had hardly the energy to argue. "But your Majesty! The green medicine . . ."

"Pondwater," said the King.

"But the blue essence!" protested the Queen, remembering the sound of her subjects quacking in the market.

"Humbug!" said the King, rising to leave. "Just like that red Elixir of Love! Nothing but pond—'

Suddenly, the Princess

Clematis gave a loud whoop. She leapt from her royal seat and ran across the room. Taking hold of Benedick by his sticky-out ears, she kissed him three times on the lips. "I'm so sorry," she said. "It must have been that Elixir of Love!" Then, with a sigh of happiness, she sank to the ground in a swoon.

"Remarkable," said the jailer. "His green medicine healed the Purple Plague."

"His yellow potion drove off the ghosts," said the Captain of the Guard.

"His blue essence turned people into ducks," said the Queen. "And now his red potion has made Clematis love him."

"And we thought he was just a quack!" said the King. "Astounding."

Benedick was just as surprised.

In the days before his wedding to Princess Clematis, Benedick was often to be seen sitting on the edge of the moat, staring into its weedy green water and shaking his head in wonder and amazement.

That is where Princess Clematis found him. She sat down at his side. "Will your family like me when they get here?

"Almost as much as I do. They will *love* their new house."

"Did you *really* kiss my

photograph each night before you went to sleep?"

"Oh, yes," said Benedick without a moment's hesitation. "I got ink on my lips, but when you're in love—"

106

"I loved you the first moment I saw you," Princess Clematis broke in. "It was very early morning, that first day you came to town. I saw you filling your bottles at the moat, below my window."

"Whoops," said Benedick.

For a while they sat in silence while the fish in the moat gulped down the greenish water.

"Do you think the Elixir of Love will ever wear off, my dear?" Princess Clematis asked.

"Oh, *never!*" said Benedick quickly.

"That's good. Because, even though your ears stick out, I like being in love with you."

"I like it too," said Benedick, honestly.

"Now, I want you to promise me one thing, dearest," said the Princess.

"Anything!" declared Benedick.

"People have a right not to be wronged."

"That's very true."

"So, after we are married . . . no more moat-water magic."

"Of course not," said Benedick meekly. "I promise."

And a duck swimming by on the moat said, *"Quack, quack, qua-ack!"*

Geraldine McCaughrean

writes books for readers of
all ages. She has won many prizes,
including the Whitbread Children's
Award (twice), the Library
Association Carnegie Medal, the
Guardian Award and the Blue Peter
Book of the Year Award.
She has also retold hundreds of
myths, legends, folktales
and literary classics.